Dear Reader,

I am proud to partner with Kohl's Cares and introduce young readers to Penguin and Bear. Each book features a universal theme that tugs at our hearts— such as losing and finding a favorite stuffed animal, feeling safe on a stormy night, making new (and sometimes unexpected!) friends on vacation, and the wonder of learning about new things. My hope is that when you share these books with the children in your life, they will feel as if they've just been given a warm hug and be inspired to discover more about the world around them.

I am passionate about childhood literacy and learning, and I am thrilled that Kohl's shares in this passion. Thank you for supporting Kohl's Cares and a lifelong love of reading for children everywhere!

Your friend,

Salina Yoon

For Max and Mason

First published in the United States of America in April 2013
by Walker Books for Young Readers, an imprint of Bloomsbury Publishing, Inc.
www.bloomsbury.com

Bloomsbury is a registered trademark of Bloomsbury Publishing Plc

For information about permission to reproduce selections from this book, write to
Permissions, Bloomsbury Children's Books, 1385 Broadway, New York, New York 10018
Bloomsbury books may be purchased for business or promotional use. For information on bulk purchases
please contact Macmillan Corporate and Premium Sales Department at specialmarkets@macmillan.com

Library of Congress Cataloging-in-Publication Data
Yoon, Salina.
Penguin on vacation / by Salina Yoon. — First U.S. edition.
pages   cm
Summary: Penguin's tired of the snow and cold—so he decides to go on vacation!
But where should he go? And what new friends will he meet along the way?
ISBN 978-0-8027-3397-9 (hardcover) • ISBN 978-0-8027-3396-2 (reinforced)
[1. Penguins—Fiction. 2. Vacations—Fiction. 3. Beaches—Fiction. 4. Friendship—Fiction.] I. Title.
PZ7.Y817Pg 2013   [E]—dc23   2012032284

ISBN 978-1-68119-170-6 (Kohl's)

Art created digitally using Adobe Photoshop • Typeset in Maiandra • Book design by Nicole Gastonguay
Printed in China by RR Donnelley Asia, Dongguan City, Guangdong
1 3 5 7 9 10 8 6 4 2

Kohl's
Style: 1681191709
Factory Number: 123386
2/16–3/16

This special edition was printed for Kohl's Department Stores, Inc.
(for distribution on behalf of Kohl's Cares, LLC, its wholly owned subsidiary)
by Bloomsbury Children's Books.

Penguin on Vacation

Salina Yoon

BLOOMSBURY
NEW YORK LONDON OXFORD NEW DELHI SYDNEY

"I need a vacation."
Penguin sighed.

Penguin had skied,

sledded,

and skated on vacations before.

He wanted to go someplace different.

Someplace . . .

"That's it! I'll go on vacation to the beach!" thought Penguin.

Penguin packed his bag
and headed north.

The waves swelled bigger and bigger.

The sun shone hotter and hotter.

Finally, Penguin reached the beach.

It wasn't what Penguin expected.

The beach was nothing like his icy home.

Penguin learned some things.

You can't ski on sand.

You can't sled on sand.

And you definitely can't skate on sand.

"Are you lost?" asked Crab.
"No, I'm on vacation,"
said Penguin.

"Then come with me!" said Crab.

Crab showed Penguin how
to have fun on the beach.

Sand castle.

Penguin and Crab played . . .

and played . . .

and played.

Penguin loved his new friend.

But all vacations come to an end.

It was time for Penguin to go home.

The journey was long and quiet,

but suddenly, something moved
in the water.

"Crab?! What are you doing here?"

"I need a vacation, too!" said Crab.

Penguin and Crab finally reached the shore.

They swam and swam.

They whooshed and pushed.

They fished and wished.

But all vacations come to an end.

Good-bye, Crab.

Crab set off for home and left behind . . .

. . . the sound of the beach.

"I shell return," wrote Crab.

So Penguin waited.

And one day, Crab did!